BEHIND THE MASK

This edition published by Parragon Books Ltd in 2014

Parragon Books Ltd
Chartist House
15–17 Trim Street
Bath BA1 1HA, UK
www.parragon.com

Writer: Joe Caramagna
Comic Artists: Scott Koblish (pages 1–7) and Giancarlo Caracuzzo (pages 8–14)
Colourist: Sotocolor
Letterer: Joe Caramagna
Cover Artists: Patrick Scherberger with Edgar Delgado
Spot Illustrations: Scott Koblish with Sotocolor and Paul Ryan,
John Romita & Damion Scott
Comic Editors: Nathan Cosby & Jordan D. White
Prose Editor: Cory Levine

ISBN 978-1-4723-4214-0

Printed in China

MARVEL
SPIDER-MAN

BEHIND THE MASK

PaRragon

Bath • New York • Cologne • Melbourne • Delhi
Hong Kong • Shenzhen • Singapore • Amsterdam

SPIDER-MAN

THE FORMER PROFESSIONAL WRESTLER TURNED SUPER HERO LEARNED THE HARD WAY THAT WITH GREAT POWER MUST COME GREAT RESPONSIBILITY. TO MAKE UP FOR HIS PAST MISTAKES, HE HAS VOWED TO PROTECT NEW YORK CITY FROM ALL THOSE WHO WISH TO DO HARM.

PETER PARKER

RAISED BY HIS UNCLE BEN AND AUNT MAY, HE ALWAYS DREAMED OF BECOMING A SCIENTIST LIKE HIS LATE FATHER. BUT AFTER A LAB ACCIDENT — AND A RADIOACTIVE SPIDER BITE — GRANTS HIM SPECIAL POWERS, HE DISCOVERS HIS TRUE CALLING.

J. JONAH JAMESON

THE PUBLISHER OF THE *DAILY BUGLE* BRINGS ATTENTION TO HIS FLOUNDERING NEWSPAPER BY GOING AFTER NEW YORK CITY'S BELOVED COSTUMED VIGILANTE.

CAPTAIN STACY

AS A VETERAN OF THE POLICE DEPARTMENT, CAPTAIN STACY KEEPS LAW AND ORDER IN NEW YORK CITY.

THE VULTURE

ADRIAN TOOMES SPENT HIS LIFE AS AN ENGINEER BUT NEVER FELT APPRECIATED BY HIS EMPLOYERS. AFTER HE WAS FIRED, HE DECIDED TO USE HIS GREATEST INVENTION, THE VULTURE HARNESS, TO GAIN THE RESPECT HE FELT HE HAD ALWAYS DESERVED.

SANDMAN

WHILE HE WAS ON THE RUN FROM THE POLICE, A CHEMICAL ACCIDENT LEFT CRIMINAL **FLINT MARKO** WITH THE ABILITY TO TURN HIS BODY INTO SAND.

DOCTOR OCTOPUS

DR OTTO OCTAVIUS WAS A WORLD-RENOWNED, YET ACCIDENT-PRONE, NUCLEAR PHYSICIST. AFTER ONE ACCIDENT TOO MANY LEFT HIM MELDED TO A SET OF FOUR ADDITIONAL MECHANICAL ARMS, HE BECAME SPIDER-MAN'S MOST FORMIDABLE SUPER VILLAIN!

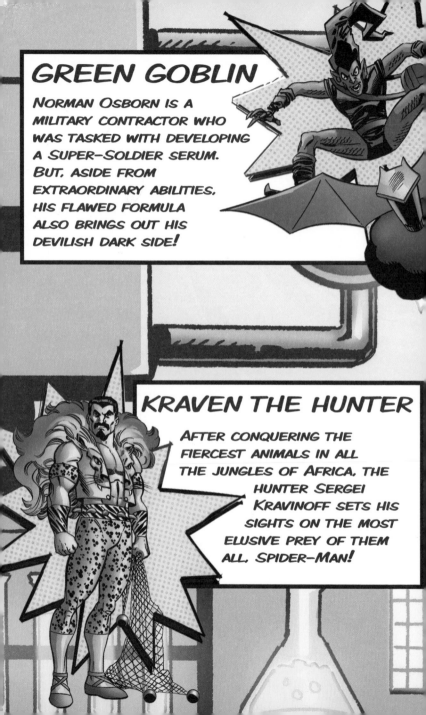

GREEN GOBLIN

NORMAN OSBORN IS A MILITARY CONTRACTOR WHO WAS TASKED WITH DEVELOPING A SUPER-SOLDIER SERUM. BUT, ASIDE FROM EXTRAORDINARY ABILITIES, HIS FLAWED FORMULA ALSO BRINGS OUT HIS DEVILISH DARK SIDE!

KRAVEN THE HUNTER

AFTER CONQUERING THE FIERCEST ANIMALS IN ALL THE JUNGLES OF AFRICA, THE HUNTER SERGEI KRAVINOFF SETS HIS SIGHTS ON THE MOST ELUSIVE PREY OF THEM ALL, SPIDER-MAN!

THE LIZARD

DR CURT CONNORS DEVELOPED A SERUM TO REPLICATE IN HUMANS A LIZARD'S ABILITY TO REGENERATE LIMBS. BUT WHEN HE TESTS IT ON HIMSELF, HE GETS MORE THAN HE BARGAINED FOR!

CHAPTER
1

One sunny morning in New York City,
mild-mannered teenager Peter Parker
walked through the early morning rush
hour with his head hanging low, but secretly
he was smiling on the inside. On any other
day, Peter would be shuffling through the
halls of Midtown High, trying not to be
noticed … but this was no ordinary day.

While other teenage boys were interested in cars and sports, Peter was content with the subway and didn't know a hockey puck from a doughnut. What Peter loved most of all were his class trips to Empire State University's science labs, where he could forget about his high-school problems and dream about what life would be like as a real-life physicist!

"Petey, Petey!" a voice called from behind.

It was his Uncle Ben trotting across the street, waving a sheet of paper.

"Petey, wait! You forgot this ... huff ... I think you need this to ... puff...," he said, out of breath. "I think you need this to get in."

"You came all this way for my permission slip?" Peter asked, taking the paper from him. "I probably could have had Mr Ditko call you—

"Oh...."

"What?"

"You signed it above 'parent' and not 'legal guardian'."

Uncle Ben blushed. Sometimes he

forgot that Peter wasn't his actual son because he and Aunt May had raised him since he was a baby. But the last thing he wanted was for Peter to think he was trying to replace his real mum and dad, who were lost in an accident many years ago.

"Oh! I'm sorry. If you have a pen, I'll fix—"

"No," Peter said as he smiled and shoved it into his rucksack. "I'm sure it'll be fine."

Uncle Ben understood, and smiled back. He thought about how much Peter had grown up since he and Aunt May first took him in. Now, 16 years later, Peter was a happy and healthy honours student who helped Aunt May with the chores and always did the right thing. He was a good boy.

"Um, Uncle Ben ..." Peter said, "... is that all?"

"Oh! Yes! I wouldn't want to embarrass you in front of your friends!" Uncle Ben waved and began his long walk back.

"Have fun, Petey! I know how much you've been looking forward to this day!"

That's right! If Peter was going to get a good spot at the radioactivity demonstration he had to hurry. He moved quickly, but as soon as he was out of Uncle Ben's sight—

"Hey, guys, look! It's 'Peeeeetey'."

Flash Thompson and two of his friends from Midtown High's football team were hanging out on the corner. Flash was the school's star quarterback, and compared to Peter, he was the size of an ox. "Is it grandpa's big day out from the old folks' home?" Flash teased.

"He's my uncle," Peter muttered and continued on his way without making eye contact.

But Flash wasn't finished yet and followed him as he walked. "Oh, that's right. I forgot," he said. "Hey, did you guys know that 'Petey' doesn't have any parents?"

Peter tried to ignore them, but the more he did, the louder Flash got.

"It's true! His parents threw themselves under a bus or something. Even they couldn't stand to be around him. Isn't that right, 'Peeeeeeetey'?"

Flash's buddies roared with laughter, but Peter didn't think it was funny at all. It was one thing to be called names like 'Pete The Science Geek' or 'Puny Parker', but this time Flash was making fun of his parents ... and Uncle Ben! He should have ignored them, but he couldn't stand to listen to any more of it.

"Shut up, Flash." And as soon as the words left his mouth, he knew he'd made a mistake. There was no way Flash would let him get away with embarrassing him in front of the football team.

"WHAT DID YOU SAY?" Flash shoved Peter so hard in the back it knocked his glasses off his face. He tried to stay on his

feet, but landed hard on the pavement.
A fireball of pain exploded from his knees.
The bullies surrounded him. Flash squeezed
his hands into fists.

"Get up!" he
shouted. "Get up and
let's see how tough
you are!"

The last thing
Peter wanted was
to have to fight
someone as big
and strong as Flash
Thompson. Instead,
he curled up on the
ground, nursing
his sore knees, and
closed his eyes and
wished the bullies
would go away,
when suddenly—

"HEY!" a
familiar voice shouted
from far away. "Leave
him alone!"

When Flash saw Uncle Ben running towards them, he stuffed his hands in his pockets and quickly walked away. "I know you! You're the Thompson boy. Eugene Thompson," Uncle Ben said. Peter had never heard anybody call Flash by his real name; even all of the teachers called him 'Flash'. "Your parents are going to hear from me when I get home."

Flash shrugged his shoulders. "He started it," he said with a wave.

Uncle Ben helped Peter to his feet. "Are you all right, Petey?" he asked. But Peter wasn't all right. He was crying.

"WHY DID YOU DO THAT?"
he shouted.

"Petey, what—?"

"If I just stay down, they get bored with it and leave me alone. But now ... I'll never be able to live this down. EVER!"

"Peter," Uncle Ben said, trying to calm him down, "you can't let guys like Thompson walk all over you like that. You have to stand up to him. If he knows you're afraid, he'll—"

"You don't know how it is, okay? Just go away!"

"But, Petey—"

"I HATE YOU!"

Uncle Ben gasped. Peter had never shouted at him like that before – it was like a punch to his gut! Peter grabbed his rucksack and ran towards the science lab as fast as he could, with his broken glasses in his hand. Uncle Ben wanted to run after him, but he knew he'd already done too much. He had embarrassed Peter in front of his classmates, but he'd only been trying to protect him. It was all he knew how to do.

CHAPTER
2

"And now, here's a brief demonstration of how we experiment with radioactivity here in the lab." Dr Lee, a physicist at Empire State University, motioned to Mr Ditko, head of Midtown High's science department, to push a button on the console in front of him. The room full of students 'oohed' and 'ahhed' as a cluster of large machines behind the safety glass beeped and buzzed with colourful lights.

"The ionization of atoms is known to cause cancer in living cells," Dr Lee said. "Hence the six-inch glass separating us from the equipment." The scientist flipped a switch and the largest machine in the room roared to life. An electrical beam zapped from one contact to the other, covering the room in a glow of blue light. Dr Lee pressed more buttons and the blue electricity crackled as the two contacts on the machine moved closer together. "But it's also been known to cause anomalies in them as well."

Usually, a scientific demonstration this remarkable would easily grab Peter Parker's attention, but he wasn't in the mood today. His glasses had been broken in the scuffle outside, so he couldn't see very well anyway, but mostly, he felt bad for yelling at Uncle Ben. He wasn't angry with him, but he was really angry at himself for letting Flash humiliate him. And every time he tried to forget about it, he heard the whispers from the back of the room.

"That old man better not say a word to my mum," said Flash.

"If I get grounded and miss the game this weekend, I'll take it out on Puny Parker for the rest of the year!"

As Dr Lee lectured, a small spider lowered itself from its web down into the energy beam between the crackling contacts. Once the beams hit it, the spider jumped wildly! It kicked its legs back and forth, but couldn't wriggle free. The blue light crackled louder and brighter.

"We experiment with bacteria, fungi, insects and arachnids ..." Dr Lee continued, "... trying to create anomalies here in the lab so we can study them to find out why they occur so that we can learn to control them."

"I say we give him a warning shot now ..." Flash said from the back of the room, "... so he knows I mean business."

Suddenly, the lights on the control panel flickered red. The machines roared louder.

"Wait, something seems to be—" Dr Lee began, but the control panel exploded in a shower of sparks! The machines began to smoke!

"Everyone get back!" Dr Lee shouted. The light flared so brightly, the students shielded their eyes.

"Come on, guys, let's get out of here,"
Flash shouted and pushed the door open.
Mr Ditko ordered the whole class to follow
him out to the car park, but Peter was
mesmerized by what was happening. This
was real science!

Suddenly – SKRASSH! – the machine
behind the window exploded, spraying the

room with a million pieces of glass! Peter put his arms in front of his face to protect himself, but he felt a sharp pinch in the back of his hand.

"OWWW!" he shrieked. Broken glass!

Except it wasn't. Peter looked at his hand and saw the little black spider that had soaked up all of the radiation in the experiment. It must have been thrown by the explosion and, in desperation, bit into the first thing that it landed on.

"Son, are you okay?" Dr Lee asked as he pulled Peter outside by the arm. Peter watched the spider stiffen and fall dead to the floor.

"Come ON!" Dr Lee shouted.

"Class, stay together while we call the paramedics," Mr Ditko said, but as his classmates gathered on the pavement, Peter kept walking.

Peter wasn't feeling well; he was dizzy and his legs felt rubbery.

"Hey, wait!" Mr Ditko shouted. "You can't leave until we make sure you're all right!"

But Peter wouldn't listen. His stomach was in knots. The spider bite on his hand throbbed. He needed to get away.

"Hey, Flash, where's Puny Parker going?" one of the bullies whispered.

"Nowhere we can't get to him. Come on," Flash said.

Across the street, Peter escaped into a secluded alley lined with bins. He felt sick to his stomach and couldn't hold it any more! He grabbed the lid off one of the bins and ...

"BLARRGGHH!"

What's happening? he wondered. Am I allergic to spider bites? Could it be—?

"What's wrong, Petey? Not feeling well?" Peter could tell by the way Flash and his buddies came into the alley that they weren't there to talk; they were there to finish what they had started. He tried to speak, but couldn't.

"Not so brave when the old man's not around, huh?" said Flash as he pounded a fist into his open palm to show Peter what he was in for.

Peter was no match for them even on a good day. But now? His legs felt brittle and he could barely stand.

He quickly looked behind him and saw plenty of room to run but didn't know if his legs could handle it. Flash reached out to grab him ... and Peter took off into the alley as fast as he could! Suddenly, his legs weren't shaky any more. They tingled. They had new life. They had power!

"GET HIM!" Flash shouted to his buddies. But the faster the bullies' legs moved, so did Peter's! Flash and his gang couldn't keep up with the new power in Peter's legs. Where was it coming from?

But when Peter turned the corner to make his final getaway, he ran straight into a fence! He was trapped and he could hear Flash's footsteps coming around the corner. He'd never be able to climb a fence this tall before Flash got to him. He was a goner for sure!

Peter felt a tingle in his knees. Time was running out. Without even thinking, he bent down deeply then pushed his trainers off the pavement with all the force he could muster.

Flash turned the corner and ran straight into the fence! His goons followed so closely behind, they ran right into his back. Flash grabbed the chain-link with his fingers and looked around, but didn't see Peter anywhere. He wasn't used to looking foolish and his face turned red with rage.

"Where did he go?" shouted Flash, but his friends just shrugged.

"He couldn't have gone too far," said one of the other bullies. "There must be some other secret way out. Yeah, that's it. Come on, Flash."

Flash turned to leave but looked over his shoulder one last time to make sure Peter wasn't just hiding somewhere. He didn't know how he'd got away, but the next time he saw him, he was going to teach him a lesson.

Meanwhile, eight metres above the ground, Peter Parker let out the big breath he had been holding to stay quiet. Way above the alley where Flash had just been, Peter clung to the side of a brick wall with just his bare hands! He couldn't explain how it had happened. With nowhere else to go, he'd jumped as high as he could – and kept going and going – right over the fence!

And when he stuck his hand out to grab on to something, it stuck to the brick wall! He placed his other hand on the wall and it stuck, too!

But after Flash left and the alley was clear, Peter was afraid to move a muscle. What if he fell to the ground and broke his arm, or worse? What if he couldn't move and was glued in place? But he couldn't just stay there all night – he had to try.

He closed his eyes and braced for the worst as he peeled his left hand away. Then, some brittle mortar broke from under the soles of his shoes and he slipped! "Whoa!" Peter shouted ... except he didn't fall! The fingers of his right hand were still firmly fixed in place, holding safely to the wall.

Peter put his left hand back on the wall and it stuck again. This time he let go with his right hand, reached up higher and stuck it back to the wall. Slowly, he was moving hand over hand, foot after foot and before he knew it, he was crawling up the wall like a bug! How is this possible? Peter wondered. And what else can I do?

"I know it hasn't been that long, but it's not like Peter not to call," Uncle Ben said quietly into the phone. "I appreciate your help anyway, Captain Stacy. I'll keep calling around."

Uncle Ben peeked his head out of the kitchen and looked over to the chair where Aunt May had been sitting for the past few hours, watching the news reports of the explosion. He'd tried to keep the phone calls quiet on account of her heart condition, but he knew by the tears in her eyes that she had been listening to him.

He couldn't give up. He scanned the list of names and phone numbers for someone – anyone – who might have seen his nephew, when he heard a sudden noise at the front door. "Peter!" he heard Aunt May say.

Uncle Ben sprang into the hallway but Peter was already sprinting up the stairs to his bedroom.

"Peter! Thank goodness!" he called out. "Where have you been? When we heard about the explosion—"

"I'm fine! I'm ... going to bed. Goodnight!" Peter shouted down the stairs before slamming his bedroom door shut.

Peter leaned his tired head against the wall and wiped the cold sweat from his forehead. So many questions swam through his mind: What was happening to him? Was it the spider bite? Was it the radiation? Was it both? Was it temporary? And – gulp – could this possibly kill him?

He pushed his microscope aside to clear some room on his desk, then grabbed a pile of pamphlets and newspaper articles from his bottom drawer and threw them down in front of him. He was looking for answers, but deep down inside he knew there wasn't a science journal in the world that could provide them. He was one of those anomalies Dr Lee had talked about.

"Um ... Peter?" a friendly voice outside of his door said with a gentle knock.

But Peter didn't dare reply. What could he say? What possible explanation could he have for where he had been all this time? Why was he pale and sweaty? There was nothing he could do but stay quiet and hope that his uncle would take the hint and go away. After all, he always could tell when Peter was lying. Or sick.

"Petey? Can you open this door, please?" Uncle Ben pleaded.

No, not sick! He couldn't be sick. He felt stronger than he had ever felt before, like he could move a mountain! And the other things he could do were amazing! Somehow, the radioactive bite gave him the proportional strength and abilities of a spider! *Let's see Flash Thompson come after me now,* Peter thought.

"Peter, can we talk about what happened?" asked Uncle Ben through the door. But Peter still ignored him.

He couldn't tell anyone about this, not even Uncle Ben and Aunt May. If anyone found out, they'd put him in a laboratory and study him like he was some kind of freak. But this was his big chance to be something more than 'Pete The Science Geek' or 'Puny Parker'. He needed a mask … and a costume. From then on he would be known as SPIDER-MAN!

CHAPTER
3

Two weeks later, Uncle Ben and Peter still hadn't talked. Uncle Ben felt bad that he had embarrassed Peter in front of his classmates, but that didn't excuse Peter for yelling at him the way that he had. Someone had to break the ice, so Uncle Ben decided to apologize for his part in it.

But every morning, Peter skipped family breakfast and then stayed out after school until the evening. When he was home, Peter locked himself in

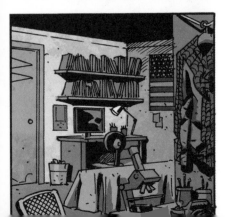

his room and didn't come out or talk
to anyone.

One night, Uncle Ben decided to give
it a shot. For 16 years they'd been the
best of friends. He couldn't
let one bad experience ruin
their relationship. "Peter?"
he said with a knock on the
locked bedroom door.

There was no answer
so Uncle Ben knocked
again. "Peter? Do you want
to watch the wrestling
match with us?" he said a
bit louder. This time he put
his ear against the door, but
there was no sound from the
other side.

Uncle Ben frowned.
"I guess you need a little
more time," he said.
"I just want you to know ...
I'm sorry about what
happened. You mean
the world to me."

But what Uncle Ben didn't know was that earlier that evening, Peter had sneaked out through his bedroom window – Uncle Ben had been talking to an empty room.

"And now, ladies and gentlemen, it's time for our MAIN EVENT!" The ring announcer proudly declared to an arena filled with rowdy wrestling fans.

"In this corner, weighing 242 pounds ... PRETTY BOY TROY!" Troy's long, dark locks shook as he bounced from foot to foot and blew kisses to the crowd that was booing him heartily. After all, Troy wasn't the man they'd paid to see.

"And his opponent—" Before he could finish his sentence, the fans howled! They were eager to see the new superstar who, in just a few short days, had taken the wrestling world by storm. The announcer pulled the microphone closer to his mouth to yell over

their cheers, "Weighing 155 pounds ...
the AMAAAAAAZING SPIDER-MAN!"

Cameras flashed all around the arena!
The spectators jumped out of their seats
as the most unusual wrestler they had ever
seen swung down from the ceiling in a
bright red and blue costume with a spider-
web pattern. Because he wore a full face
mask,nobody had any idea that this wrestler
was really just teenage science student,
Peter Parker!

When the bell sounded, Pretty Boy
Troy lunged from his corner to catch the
fan-favourite by surprise, but Spider-Man
side-stepped him with ease, sending Troy
face-first into the opposite corner. Troy
turned around and threw a heavy punch,
but again Spider-Man dodged the strike
with a high jump. He was by far the most
agile fighter the adoring crowd had ever
seen! When Spider-Man pushed Troy down
to the mat with a kick to the star on the seat
of his wrestling trunks, the fans roared with
laughter! Troy, very embarrassed, sprang
back up to his feet, made sure his hair was

still in place, then lunged again! But Spider-Man kicked the handsome wrestler in the stomach and knocked the wind right out of him!

"Take it easy, kid," Troy grunted. "You really hurt me that time!"

But the fans weren't there to see him take it easy, and urged him on, chanting, "Spidey! Spidey!"

"But listen to them! They're eating it up!" Spider-Man said. He jumped high over Troy's head and landed on the other side of him. When he turned round, Spider-Man dropkicked him in the chest, sending Troy hard into the corner of the ring! "And speaking of 'eating', what did you eat today? Your breath smells like you brushed your teeth with kitty litter!"

Before Troy could reply, Spider-Man pressed a small button in the palm of his hand, and stringy, sticky gloop – like a spider's web – sprayed from his own special invention, a web-shooting bracelet hidden beneath his red and blue gloves. The webbing went all over Troy's mouth! He grabbed at it, but it stuck to him like glue. Spidey, still holding the other end of the web, yanked it hard over his shoulder, lifting Troy right up off the mat and clear over the ropes. Troy fell hard onto the floor!

The match was over! Spider-Man was the winner! The audience thundered in applause and chanted, "Spidey! Spidey!" Underneath the mask, Peter Parker smiled with delight. Everyone in the stadium adored him!

Well, almost everyone. Pretty Boy Troy, his face covered in webs, struggled to get up to his feet. For the first time in his long wrestling career he was made to look like a fool.

Spider-Man didn't wrestle the way they had planned and he had humiliated Troy just to make himself look better.

"But, Mr Barnaby ... that's not fair!"

"Life ain't fair. You know the rule, kid," said the wrestling promoter, as he removed large stacks of money from a pile on his desk and dropped them into a laundry bag. "I'm not paying you until I get your real name on a real contract."

"But my identity is a secret! Nobody can ever find out who I really am!"

"Sorry, Spidey," Barnaby shrugged, "but

you don't get what you want until I get what I want."

A caretaker who was in the promoter's office mopping the floor, couldn't help but overhear. The scar over his left eye bounced as he cackled. He'd never seen such a big pile of cash after just one show and he knew a shrewd promoter like Mr Barnaby wasn't going to give that up quite so easily.

Mr Barnaby slipped on his dark glasses and laughed along with him. Their laughter reminded Peter of Flash Thompson and his buddies, and Peter couldn't stand it. Even now, after all the great things he could do, they still treated him like 'Puny Parker'.

In a rage, Spider-Man grabbed Mr Barnaby by the collar of his flashy jacket and lifted the heavy man high into the air with ease. The caretaker suddenly didn't think it was so funny any more and went back to taking out the rubbish.

"I won't be bullied ever again!" said Spider-Man. "Pay me what you owe me!"

"All right, f-fine. T-take your share. Just don't hurt me!" Barnaby said.

That felt good, Peter thought, as he strutted down the hall from Mr Barnaby's office in his Spider-Man costume. For the first time in his life, he'd stood up for himself. And after the match, the fans, the money and his newfound nerve ... it had been a great day.

"E-excuse me, Spider-Man," a young man said from the lift doors. Except it wasn't just any young man ... it was Flash Thompson! And his bully buddies were with him! Only now, next to Spider-Man, they looked shorter and uncertain. They looked weak. "Can I have y-your autograph?"

Spider-Man looked at the pen and paper in Flash's hand, but didn't take it. He decided to have some fun instead.

"I know you," he said, disguising his voice so they wouldn't recognize him. "You're that quarterback who took Midtown

High to the state championship.
Flash Thompson!"

Flash's eyes lit up! "Yeah! That's me!"
he said, standing up taller and more
confidently. Now he looked more like the
bully Peter knew so well. "We almost won
that game, too!"

"Almost?" Spider-Man mocked.
"Sorry, kid ..."

With a mere flick of his wrist,
using great spider-strength, Spider-Man
shoved Flash hard into the lift buttons on
the wall. "Ooof!"

"... but I don't sign autographs
for losers."

The lift doors opened wide, but before Spider-Man could get in, he heard someone down the hall shout, "HEY! STOP HIM!"

Spider-Man and Flash turned to see the caretaker running towards them from Mr Barnaby's office. In one hand was the laundry bag full of money and in his other hand ... a gun! Mr Barnaby was chasing after him, but couldn't keep up.

"Pardon me," the caretaker said as he slipped past the teenagers and into the open lift. As the doors closed, Spider-Man watched the scar above the thief's eye bounce with laughter again as he escaped.

"What's the matter with you?" Mr Barnaby shouted at the web-slinger. "Couldn't you just trip him or grab him or something?!"

"Sorry, Mr Barnaby," he answered. "Life ain't fair." As Peter walked away from Mr Barnaby, Flash Thompson and the bullies, he smiled under his mask again. *This isn't just a great day*, he thought. *It's the greatest day of my life!*

CHAPTER 4

Peter put his regular clothes on over his
Spider-Man costume and stuffed the mask
and his winnings from the match into his
pocket for the walk home from the arena.
It was the first time in a long time that he
was proud to be himself again. *Oh, if only*

Uncle Ben could have seen that, he thought. *He would have been so proud!*

But Peter hadn't spoken to Uncle Ben since the confrontation with Flash at the university. So many exciting things had happened since then, but without Uncle Ben to share them with, they seemed a little less ... special. He decided that when he got home, he'd apologize for the way he'd acted. *Actually,* thought Peter, *I should tell him all about it – the spider, the powers, the wrestling – everything. I bet he'd get a real kick out of it.*

But when Peter rounded the corner to his street, he saw two police cars and an ambulance parked in front of his apartment building!

It gave him a very bad feeling in his gut. It must be Aunt May's heart! "Aunt May! Uncle Ben!" he shouted, pushing past some people who had gathered out the front. Peter ran for the door, but a large police officer with a bushy moustache stretched out his arm to block his path.

"Whoa! Sorry, son, you can't go in there!"

"Where's my aunt?" Peter asked.

"Oh! You must be Peter! I'm Officer Keating. We've been calling all over for you."

"Where's Aunt May?" Peter repeated.

Officer Keating placed his hands on Peter's shoulders. "Your Aunt May is fine, son. She's over at the Watsons' house." Peter put his hand over his heart and let out a sigh of relief. But Officer Keating didn't look as relieved. If Aunt May was over at the Watsons' then where was—

"Uncle Ben?" Peter asked.

Officer Keating bowed his head. Peter's heart started beating so loudly, he could barely make out the policeman's words.

It was a burglar. He had a gun.

Uncle Ben thought Peter was asleep in his room and had tried to protect him. The gun went off and—

The officer looked away. Peter collapsed inside. His arms and legs trembled. His eyes filled with tears. He couldn't believe it. Uncle Ben was gone. He was really gone. All because he was trying to protect Peter.

"But don't worry," Officer Keating continued as he gripped Peter's shoulders tightly. "We found the guy. We've got him cornered in an old warehouse on the waterfront.

"Now, you'd better go see your Aunt May. She's worried sick about you. There's nothing you can do here."

Officer Keating was right, there was nothing Peter Parker could have done. But Spider-Man can do all kinds of amazing things.

The old, empty warehouse on the Hudson River came alive in the glow of the flashing red lights of a dozen police cars. A lifetime on the job had taught Captain George Stacy to stay patient during times like this, so he ordered his officers to surround the building and keep their distance.

The burglar inside had a gun and was willing to use it. Captain Stacey would try everything he could to draw the burglar out before risking anyone's safety with a raid.

"Don't be foolish," Captain Stacy said, his voice amplified through the night sky by a megaphone. "There's nowhere for you to go. Come out peacefully and I promise you won't be hurt."

Inside the warehouse, the burglar wiped away the dust from a dirty old window and saw that Captain Stacy was right – there were police officers everywhere. But he knew as long as he stayed put, he'd be safe. Nobody would dare come after him, would they?

The burglar's eyes jumped as a sudden creaking sound came from the shadows in the ceiling's rafters. He raised his gun slowly. Were there policemen on the roof? Was Captain Stacy just a distraction? Suddenly a voice called out:

"MURDERER!"

The burglar spun round and blindly fired his gun twice into the darkness! Without knowing if he'd hit anything, he ran away as fast as he could, but a figure in red and blue dropped from out of the shadows to block his path! It was Spider-Man!

The burglar quickly aimed his gun but Spider-Man was even faster.

CRICK!

While the burglar squeezed the trigger
again and again, Spidey jumped from the
wall to the floor and back again, avoiding
the gunshots. He tried to fire again, but
Spider-Man sprayed webbing from his
web-shooter and smothered the burglar's
gun in the goo.

   "No," Spider-Man said, "you're not
hurting anyone else tonight!"

The burglar tried to run but Spider-Man yanked the web-line and pulled him back! "Never again!" he yelled.

He punched the burglar across the jaw! Then again across his cheek! Then a final uppercut blow to his chin! The burglar stumbled backwards, woozy, but Spider-Man wasn't finished with him yet. He threw him

up against a wall in
the moonlight to get
a better look at the
man who had
killed his uncle.

And that's
when Peter saw
the burglar's scar. The
same scar from Mr Barnaby's
office. Over the caretaker's eye. The
same caretaker who stole the bag full of
money. The same caretaker
that Peter let escape into the
lift because he was too
busy getting revenge
on Flash Thompson.
That same caretaker
had shot Uncle Ben.

Peter dropped to
the floor, then pulled
the spider-mask from
his face and began to
cry. What a
fool he had
been! If he

had stopped him earlier when he took Mr Barnaby's money, the caretaker would have been behind bars and unable to do what he'd done to Uncle Ben. It was all Peter's fault!

Outside, Captain Stacy crawled out from behind a police car. He hadn't heard gunshots from inside the building for several minutes, so he felt it was safe to get back up. Slowly. He wasn't sure what had happened, but he held a finger to his mouth to make sure the officers stayed quiet as he tried to listen for any movement.

Suddenly, something big crashed through the window and landed hard on the pavement in front of the police. Captain Stacy and a few officers ran over and saw that it was the burglar; he was wrapped from head to toe in what looked like a thick spider's web!

Who could have done this? the captain wondered. And when he looked up into the sky, he saw exactly who – that professional wrestler he had seen on television, the Spider-Man! He watched him swing away on a web and disappear into the Manhattan skyline.

Three days later, a long black car pulled to the kerb in front of the Parkers' apartment building. Peter, wearing a suit and tie, stepped out first and reached back to take the outstretched hand of Aunt May, who was catching her tears in a handkerchief. It was all over. Uncle Ben was gone. Now it was time for Peter to start his new life as the man of the house.

After much thinking, Peter realized he was wrong to think Uncle Ben would have been proud of the way he'd acted. By using his new abilities to overpower Flash Thompson and Mr Barnaby, he was no better than they were. He was being selfish and had learned the hard way that with great power must come great responsibility. To make it up to Uncle Ben, he had to put things right.

Peter heard the distant wail of a police siren. Something was happening.

Now wearing his red and blue Spider-Man costume, he climbed out of his bedroom window and into the alley. He touched his fingers to the wall and began to climb to the roof to get a look at where the police were headed. His uncle was right: in times of trouble, he couldn't stay down, he had to stand up. New York City needed someone with his special gifts to help make sure what had happened to Uncle Ben would never happen to anyone else. New York City needed a hero like Spider-Man!